Lu's
Outing

John Lugo-Trebble

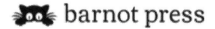 barnot press

2020 edition published by barnot press.

Contact: john@johnlugotrebble.net

ISBN:
978-1-9160596-0-3

DEDICATION

To my husband David:

Your belief in me lit the way during the dark times when I
didn't even believe in myself.
Thank you.

To my mother Mirta and my siblings Joey, Elisa and
Kasandra for always loving me for who I am.

To Boots: Forever Missed.

ACKNOWLEDGMENTS

I would like to thank my friends who I consider my family for the times we have had and the friendships we have cultivated over the years.

I would also like to thank the NYC I grew up in for inspiring this story and for the times we had in the 90's.

AUTHORS NOTE

Lu's Outing began as a short story when we were living in Prague in 2013. I was sitting in *Q Cafe* in Nové Město. The doors were wide open and there was no breeze. I looked at the sweat beads forming on my arm and was transported back to the humid summers of my youth in NYC.

I wrote most of it in one sitting. The finished product fell somewhere between a short story and a novel so it sat in a folder until 2018.

The summer of 2018 was overshadowed by the tragic loss of our beloved cat Boots and I needed a project to focus my grief on. I decided to enter *Lu's Outing* in the Amazon Storyteller Competition and although it didn't win the contest, it did gain a following.

This 2020 revised edition contains never published material. It also sets the stage for the second instalment in Lu's Adventure, *The Deadbeat Club* (Spring 2020).

In addition to Spanglish, *Lu's Outing* uses language and terminology that was common at the time but today not so much. It presents a time in LGBTQ+ history where we were becoming more visible but the law had yet to catch up.

It is not my coming out story, but if I had to choose one...

THURSDAY, JUNE 2, 1993

It didn't bother me that I was all those names they called me: Sissy, Fag, Mama's Boy, Butt Pirate! It hurt that it bothered them so much. Well the last name bothered me because I hadn't actually done that yet. I hadn't done anything. I was a virgin. The closest I had come to a man were the few copies of *Male Pictorial* I had stashed under my mattress. I had taken them from Uncle Jose's apartment when we cleaned it out after he died. My mother didn't want *abuela* to "see those things." Instead of throwing them in the garbage, I stashed them in my school bag, looking forward to getting home that night and flipping through them. Those magazines became my nightly escape. "Ian" in particular became a fixation. Smooth, golden skin,

1

honey like dirty blond hair and piercing blue eyes, with strong arms that I would imagine wrapped around me. His body was manly. Next to his, mine was way underdeveloped; skinny and boyish.

My head against the conductor's booth, I was daydreaming about "Ian" while listening to "In Your Room" by The Bangles on the 80's mixed tape that I had made the night before. I could feel that familiar dread starting to rise in my stomach as the train pulled into the nearest stop to my high school. The sky was too blue for abuse, so instead of getting on the bus at Pelham Bay, I hopped the 6 train and decided to go downtown with no real idea where I was going. The doors opened and shut with indifference and as it pulled away from Middletown Road, I would be safe from *them*, even if only for one day.

I stayed on the train to Astor Place. With no destination in mind, I walked around Washington Square Park. I used to hear Mom say to Uncle Jose to be careful around there because of all the drug dealers and addicts. Looking around all I saw were people who looked pretty average to me. Some my age who were probably playing hooky too and others a bit older probably going to classes at NYU. There were all sorts of men playing chess in one corner of the park. I felt safer than I did at school. Looking through the arch in the park, the haze in the city made it hard to see the Empire State Building clearly. My arms were a bit sweaty and the light blond hairs glistened just above my olive skin.

I headed towards Eighth Street, turning left and passing by the *8th Street Playhouse* that had a big sign advertising *The Rocky Horror Picture Show*. I had seen it on TV late one night when my mom had some friends over and she thought I had gone to bed early. I hummed "Sweet Transvestite" in my head for days. It even provided a distraction when Anthony Diagio punched me repeatedly in the stomach for walking too close to him. *How cool would it be to see it at the movies?*

Eighth Street was lined with shop after shop selling variations of the same things: bongs, pipes, t-shirts, shoes and ear piercings. Towards Sixth Avenue there

were two black drag queens outside of a shop called
Patricia Fields. They had corsets like Frankenfurter and
the biggest heels I had ever seen in my life. One of
them had on a red bobbed wig and the other one a
blonde ponytail. I remember Uncle Jose wearing a
similar pony tail when he dressed up as Madonna the
last Halloween that he was alive. Even sick as he was,
he insisted on celebrating. My mother made sure none
of his lesions were visible through the foundation she
used on his neck.

The blonde one exhaled from her cigarette and then
said to the red headed one, "Ah told that mothafucka
don't be holding my head I ain't yo wife!!"

I tried not to laugh as I walked past. It made me miss
Uncle Jose more than I had done in a while. I walked
past *Papaya King* and crossed Sixth Avenue when I
noticed the sign that said Christopher Street. I used to
hear Uncle Jose talk about this place to my mother.
Smoking his *Newport*, he would cross his legs; pointing
his finger at my mom as he spoke.

"*Tienes que salir con migo chica, vamos al Christopher Street*...we have a good time."

Mom would laugh it off. "*Chico, no hay nada para mi en el village.*"

I headed down Christopher Street and noticed a bookshop on the right called *Oscar Wilde*. I was intrigued so I slowed down just outside of it. I paced back and forth, looking around as if I had stopped to check my watch. I pushed the door and entered quickly as if Diagio had been chasing me down the street at that very moment. The guy behind the counter smiled as I walked in. He must've seen me acting like an idiot before entering the shop. My face felt like it was on fire as I took in the sight of him. He was maybe in his 20's I think, and slim. Not skinny like me but slim, like underneath his mustard brown t-shirt there was a chest that had definition; unlike mine. He had ear length dirty blond hair; a little darker than "Ian's" which was pushed to one side and gave his brown eyes softness, like you could tell he was a nice guy. The way he looked at me made me feel like I was the only person in the world. In a gentle voice he said, "Give me a shout if you need any help."

I smiled, shook my head and thought to myself, *Oh I'd want more than a shout.* I then looked at the shelves for something other than him to focus on. I settled on a copy of *Giovanni's Room* by James Baldwin. Mrs. Perez never mentioned he was gay when she taught us about him. Names I had heard about in school jumped off the shelves; EM Forrester, Virginia Woolf and Langston Hughes. I pulled out a book that caught my eye. *Reflections of a Rock Lobster* by Aaron Fricke. Four other books fell off the shelf at the same time. I looked at the guy behind the counter embarrassed and I dropped to the ground trying to pick up the books, all the while apologising. He came over and patted my shaking body.

"No worries, accidents happen." He said and winked at me. His touch sent a shock down my spine and found its way to my crotch. My face started to burn again.

"I'm sorry."

"Don't worry your pretty self." He put the books back on the shelf and stood there in front of me, his eyes looked me over and my head spun from the attention.

"Thanks." *He called me pretty.*

"What's your name?"

"Luis, but everyone calls me Lu." I responded. *Liar, nobody calls you anything nice.*

"Cool. I'm Si."He held his hand out and as my hand met his, another pulse of energy shot through me again.

"Nice to meet you."

"Likewise." He smiled back. "So, you playing hooky?" He asked.

Now I was really embarrassed. "Is it that obvious?" My cheeks were still on fire.

He giggled. "A little." His hands were now in his pocket and he was rocking back and forth kind of nervous. Though I wasn't entirely sure why. "I finish at 4. Wanna grab a coffee?"

"Yes. I mean yea, sure." I said not containing my excitement and feeling like a total dork.

His face lit up. "Cool, so meet me here at 4."

"Okay, cool. Can I pay for this?" I asked holding a copy of *Reflections of a Rock Lobster*.

"Take it. It's on me." He responded.

"No. I couldn't." I reached into my pocket but he stopped me.

"Seriously, it's worth a read. Anyway most of the guys who come in here just buy the porn mags. Nice to have a customer who reads." He winked.

I thanked him for the book; already looking forward to four o' clock. I left *Oscar Wilde*; there were still a few hours before the cops would stop looking for truants. I remember hearing that bitch Melanie Sputano saying something about them not looking after 2.30. Maybe she was right? I know she wasn't right about other things. "Oh Anthony, Luis is looking at your butt." I hadn't been. I was lost in thought and staring off into space. It didn't matter though; Diagio still punched me as she laughed.

I walked down towards Sheridan Square and saw a diner off the side street that looked from the outside as if it had seen better days, *Tiffany's* it was called. I crossed over but before I could reach the door I was interrupted.

"*Papi*, you don't want to go in there." I turned to face a guy, maybe my age, maybe older. It was hard to tell with the jet black bobbed wig and red lipstick which accentuated his mocha skin.

"Oh Gurl, this one is cute." His friend said. He was an effeminate and handsome black guy who was wearing baggy blue jeans and a crisp white tank top which made his skin look gorgeous. The tone of his upper body didn't match his voice. "The pigs usually come in here looking for truants." He continued.

I was stopped in my tracks. *Fuck.* "Thanks."

9

They looked at each other then back at me. "Child, where you going?"

I looked around, not sure of where to go. I shrugged my shoulders. They walked up to me and grabbed me from either side, placing one arm around my arm, pulling me around the corner in the direction of Christopher Street.

"Where are we going?"

"Pier gurl." Said the one in the wig.

"I'm James." The effeminate black guy introduced himself.

"I'm Cuchi Frita. At least when the wig is on."

"What about when the wig is off?" I asked.

"I'm someone else." Cuchi teased.

"Oh. Ok. I'm Lu." I said.

James and Cuchi looked at one another. "Lu?"

"Yea, it's short for Luis."

James nodded his head. "We'll work on that honey."

"Mmhmm" Cuchi responded in agreement.

We walked down Christopher Street arm in arm, past gay shops, gay people, rainbow flags, as if there was nothing else in the world but gays. I felt like I was in a dream. I saw two guys walking up the opposite side of the street. They were holding hands and had their heads held high. No one flinched, no one took notice, and no one shouted. No one cared. Everyone and everything around me felt brighter than the blinding sun on that warm day.

"I remember the first time I walked down Christopher Street too." James said to me.

"What?" I answered, interrupted from the dream like state I was in.

He continued, "Being amazed, feeling like I had just come home."

"Mmhmm" Cuchi added.

I smiled.

"It'll pass honey" They both laughed. I didn't
understand why they were laughing. Their words fell
like anchors in my heart. I didn't want it to pass. I
wanted to feel like this forever.

"Oh James, let huh enjoy the moment." Cuchi said,
perhaps sensing my confusion. We had only just met
but I could already tell from their humor and
mannerisms that they were years ahead of me; even
though we were about the same age. *Is this what happens
with experience?* I thought to myself.

Walking past the entrance to the PATH train there
was a breeze that provided a momentary relief from
the heat, albeit a smelly one. Beyond that the street
widened and before us I could see the Hudson which
looked refreshing in this weather.

"First time down here honey?" James asked.

"Yea"

"Well gurl, stick with us. Bitches down here will chew you up and spit you out."

"Or make you spit." James added.

"*Ay* James, you're so bad."

The double act was at it again.

We crossed the West Side Highway and walked past little clusters of Latino and Black kids, some in wigs, some dressed like the gangster boys in my block and others who could have been either boys or girls. One of the tough looking guys whistled in our direction and called out, "pssss pssss *Papi*. How you doing?" I looked over; he blew a kiss and winked.

"Carlos, you better keep your motherfucking diseased dick away okay *cabron*." Cuchi yelled out, grabbing my arm tighter.

The clusters of people became one with laughter. Little words rose above the noise like "oh snap....no she didn't...you better werk Cuchi."

"I told you that shit cleared up. Why you gotta be like that?" He then dismissed us with a wave.

We walked on and I couldn't help but feel good about the attention I was getting. At school, unless it was to call me a name or chase after me, I wandered the halls a spirit; a nobody. Someone you walked into without looking at and forgot to say "excuse me" to.

"You gotta watch out for motherfuckers down here." James said to me. "Cute, young thing like you."

Cute? I'm cute. I've never been called cute. I couldn't contain my excitement.

"Everything happens for a reason *Luisito*." Cuchi then added. *Not even my mother called me that.* The warm breeze blew a few strands of her wig across her face and she brushed them away as we walked onto the Pier. "I know you *Papi*. You get called all sorts of names at school. The girls don't look at you. The boys can't look at you. You come down here and suddenly you a star baby. I saw you smile when Carlos called out to you."

I felt like I was getting a lecture from my mother.

"Each day there is a you that comes down here for the first time, and a Carlos waiting to take advantage. But when you with us, no motherfucker will hurt you. We have to look out for each other. ¿*Sabes?*"

I nodded my head in agreement. There was something in the tone of how she said those words that made me believe her. It made me feel safe, like I belonged for the first time. I wondered if I should mention Si and coffee later. *What if Si was like Carlos? No. I mean it was obvious he was a nice guy, right?*

"Oh let's sit here" James said, not waiting for a response just plopping down against the right side of the Pier in front of the warning sign on the fence. I could see a few guys sunbathing naked on the other side, as if they didn't care or didn't notice that that part of the Pier was falling into the river. I found it difficult not to notice them. Apart from myself, the only other naked guys I had ever seen were in the magazines under my bed. I hadn't even seen a dirty movie yet.

15

The sun was shining bright but the temperature was a bit cooler being out that far from the street. The pier looked as if it could collapse at any moment and yet looking around at all the different types of people hanging out without a care in the world, there was sense of belonging. A sense of home.

"Thanks." I said to both of them.

"For what?" James responded.

I looked at them both, trying to find the strength to say the words without sounding cheesy. "For bringing me down here."

"Ay, we got a sentimental one here." Cuchi teased. She ruffled my hair like I was a kid and smiled.

We talked for hours like we had known each other for years. Cuchi still refused to tell me her name out of drag.

"Don't worry *Papi*, you'll meet him soon enough." She said. "Cuchi's the fun one though."

"Mmmhmmm" James looked at her. "Still the same shady bitch with or without make up."

I laughed and Cuchi gave me a nasty look like some upset diva on a *telenovela.*

"Gurl, don't be acting all hurt." James said. "You know you are."

"I know right?" She responded.

Cuchi was from The Bronx too but moved to Manhattan when she was 10. She went to a Catholic school and had come out two years ago when she was 14. We were the same ages but at the same time, years apart.

James was from Brooklyn, went to Stuyvesant, which was the best public school in the city and had come out only a year ago at 16. They weren't surprised I hadn't come out and listened to me as I spoke about how much I hated going to school and how I missed my Uncle Jose. I had never told anyone else that he died of HIV related Pneumonia. I never had anyone to tell. I never even mentioned it out loud. Even now,

mom rarely mentioned his name and when she did it
was to remember a funny memory. Guess it was easier
to laugh than cry. It felt good to talk about him; a relief
even.

I glanced at my watch, nearly 4pm. "Shit, I have to
go."

"Alright *Papi*, you want us to walk you to the train?"
Cuchi asked with concern in her voice.

"No it's cool."

I went to get up and James said, "What no kiss
goodbye?"

He leant over and planted his soft lips on my cheek.
I returned the gesture. Then I kissed Cuchi. I still had
a lot to learn. I got up and then thought about how I
would see them again.

"Wait, when will I see you two again?"

James without thinking said, "Come to *The Center* on
13th and 7th this Saturday, about 2. We're always
there."

"How will I know it's *The Center*?"

"*Papi*, there'll be a crowd of loud queens in front of it and a big ol' rainbow flag."

"Oh okay."

I walked back towards the West Side Highway. Carlos paid me no mind this time. He had a young black guy in his arms who was giggling and smiling; lost in the attention. I felt a little guilty about lying to Cuchi and James about where I was going. They had been nothing but nice to me. *What if I was wrong about Si being a nice guy?* I shook the thought out of my head and thought about Si's soft brown eyes and the smile that made my stomach jump. I felt a spring in my step as I crossed the street.

Walking up Christopher Street on my own I walked tall; just like everyone else. I could never do that at school. I smiled at people. It felt good when they smiled back or winked at me. Although I didn't know what was coming next, I knew for sure that I was not the same kid that decided that morning to play hooky. No, Luis Morales would never be *that* kid again.

As soon as I walked past Sheridan Square, I could see the golden streaks in Si's hair glistening in the sun coming through breaks in the trees that lined the street. He was sitting on a stoop reading a worn out paperback. As I got closer, I saw the title, *Les Miserables.* He looked up, smiled as he got up and said, "Hey Lu." It was like the sun beaming right back at me. He put the paperback in the back pocket of his baggy brown cargos and put his hand on my shoulder. His touch felt electric and I could feel the heat rising in my face.

"Hey." I said.

"Nice to see you again." We walked back the direction I had just come.

"How was the rest of your day?" I asked.

"A few guys came in. Usual I guess. You?"

"Walked down to the Pier." I felt a ball in my stomach form as the words left my lips.

"Be careful down there, not for everyone." Concern in his voice more than judgement.

I shrugged my shoulders. "It was okay. I had a drag queen protecting me."

"A drag queen bodyguard and a date? Having quite the day so far." He smirked.

He called it a date. I was on a date. I didn't imagine it. He actually said date. I blushed. The afternoon was even brighter than the day had been.

The streets were full of people walking up and down. A few stood around as if they were the only ones that mattered. Then as if a balloon had popped; I heard her voice.

"Well, well, James, *mira esto?*"

"Mmmmhmmm *escandalo!*"

They were standing in front of us. I was frozen with fear. I felt like I was found out by my mother and about to be grounded. I could almost feel the sting of the *chancleta* against my skin.

"I thought you were going home?" She asked; her eyes wide open as she stared down at me.

"Oh Lu. Out of all the drag queens, you found this one?" Si said as he stepped around and examined Cuchi from top to bottom.

"Ooh" James cooed, "This one is shady!"

Without looking away from me, she held her hand up at Si. "Did I address you trade?"

"A dress? You should try one some time. You might even pass."

Cuchi took a step back. James shook his head in disbelief. "Oh trade is throwing shade."

I didn't know what was going on and just when I was about to say something, they all looked at one another, then me and started laughing.

Cuchi grabbed me. "Ay gurl, you so serious..*pobrecito*. She then turned to Si, "hey baby, how are you?"

"You know each other?" I asked. I was confused by what had just happened.

"Cuchi, knows errybody." James said.

"And been with them too." Si added.

"*Degraciadas*." Cuchi sneered back.

She then pulled me aside. "I'm sorry..." She put her finger up to my lip. The red nail polish was beginning to crack.

"*Luisito*, you get one of those. Don't lie to mama, she always finds out."

I nodded. "I didn't want you to make fun of me."

"Honey, out here, excuses can get you hurt. You're young, beautiful and there are a lot of creepy motherfuckers out there, you hear me."

I looked over at Si who was talking to James, then back at Cuchi. "Him?"

"He's one of the good ones. You got lucky."

"I hope to." I smiled back.

She put her hand on her chest. "Your first come back!"

"Proud?" She nodded her head in agreement. She then pulled me close to her with a huge hug and whispered, "Have fun on your date. See you Saturday."

She pulled away from me and said, "Simon, you better be good to huh. Make sure she shows up on Saturday." She then snapped her finger, "James, come on, I have a French essay to finish. *Au revoir* bitches!"

They walked on. I looked at Si who held his hand out towards me. I placed my hand in his. Our palms were sweaty but it felt nice. He gently squeezed my hand as we walked in to a place called *The Espresso Bar*. It was long and narrow with seats against the wall to the left and a long counter to the right. I felt like the whole room was looking at us as we walked in.

We approached the counter and there were sounds of "hey Si" coming from all directions. Si leant over and gave the guy a peck on the cheek. "Hey Baby."

"Hey Honey." Like James, his voice did not match the muscles on his arms or the pecs that seemed to want to break through his tight black t-shirt. Nothing was exactly what it seemed down here in the village.

Si introduced us. His name was Todd. I smiled feeling inadequate. Todd was gorgeous, like the guys in the pages of *Male Pictorial* that I had stashed under my mattress at home. *Why was Si holding my hand and not his?*

"What can I get you boys?"

"Usual for me..."

"And you honey?"

"Ummm." I couldn't read the menu clearly because Todd's broad shoulders were in the way but I smelled hazelnut so I ordered one of those.

"Right then, two hazelnuts Lamal." He called out. Lamal acknowledged us with a smile. "Take a seat boys, I'll bring them over to you." *We even like the same coffee! That's a sign, right?*

"Thanks baby." Si responded. I felt so unworthy of *Mr. Cool* here holding my hand.

We walked towards the back, past the bathroom and onto a small patio, his hand in mine the entire time. *How could I feel so here yet so out of place at the same time?*

We sat down at a small table, our knees brushed against one another. Si kept smiling at me. I felt on the spot. *Silence. Smile.* Nerve wracked, like I needed to go to the toilet. I took a deep breath.

"So you from the city?" I asked.

He shook his head. "No, I was born in Paris."

"Oh you're French. I would love to go to Paris one day."

He smiled. "I'm not. I was born there, raised in England till I was 10, then we came here."

"Oh, why so?"

"My dad got a job transfer and my mom was homesick."

"So your mom is American and your dad is..."

"Cornish...."

"I have no idea what you just said."

He leaned in closer. "I won't tell my dad you said that when you meet him." He then winked.

It turned out Cornwall is in the UK but not England; at least to the Cornish it wasn't. I told Si about my own background which was summed up as *Nuyorican* born and raised in The Bronx, it wasn't a long or exciting story.

Our coffees arrived as Si asked me how old I was.

"Umm 17."

His eyebrows arched. "Really?"

"In September."

He squeezed my hand. "Thought so...junior?"

"Yea and you?"

"18"

"Freshman?"

"Ouch. Why not high school senior?"

"Because you wouldn't be working in a bookstore during the day." I said.

"Clever and cute."

I took a sip of my coffee feeling embarrassed, which he picked up on. Yet his reassurances of my good looks could not take away what I faced everyday at school; although for a moment he did make me feel like Molly Ringwald at the end of *Sixteen Candles*. Si was studying French Literature at NYU which is why he was reading *Les Miserables*. It wasn't just a musical. *I was happy I kept that to myself.* He was living at home on the Upper West Side but hoping to move downtown his second year. Our worlds were so opposite.

"I've never been to The Bronx." He said

"I hate it."

"Why?"

I looked around me, as if I someone was listening in and I was about to divulge some great secret."I don't fit in."

He smiled in a way that made me look down and then up at him. "At your age, you don't fit in anywhere."

"I feel like I fit in here."

He took my hand. "It's the Village, we're all misfits here."

It was nearly 5pm when we left *Espresso Bar*. Si wanted to walk me up to *The Center* but all I could picture was my mother's face as I walked through the door late and without an excuse.

"It's on the way." He held out his hand.

I couldn't resist. We walked up 7th Avenue South towards 13th Street hand in hand. The sun was still shining and I felt as if I were floating; my feet weren't touching the ground. When we got to the corner of 13th Street, he pointed to a tree lined street, opposite us. The prettiest street I had seen. "One day I am going to live there." He said. The way his eyes looked beyond what was in front of him made me believe he would.

"It's beautiful."

"There's a converted church down there. That's my dream home."

I squeezed his hand which brought his attention back to the moment. He squeezed it back and we turned towards a building that looked like a school with a rainbow flag outside of it.

"Well, that's it." Si said.

"Cool." *Ugh, why cool, again?*

We walked towards it and when we got in front, we stopped. I looked up at the sign. Si grabbed my other hand and stood in front of me. Looking into my eyes and as if in slow motion, he leaned in towards me. His smile was replaced with a softness I found hard to describe but it sent a shiver through my body and the moment felt serious; good serious not bad serious. His lips touched mine. My body shook. I put my arms around him and pulled him close, unsure of how I knew to do that. It felt natural. It felt right. I tilted my head and pressed my lips harder against his, feeling his breath as his mouth opened and my tongue met his. My head exploded with the sound of fireworks as I got hard. I could feel that it was mutual.

"Ooooooooooh child, to be young again...mmhmm."

I opened my eyes and there were two older guys looking at us, beaming with smiles as if they were two proud grandparents who had a mischievous streak.

"Please honey, you were NEVER *that* young." The other one said.

Si and I looked at each other and laughed. The moment had become more funny than intimate.

"Oh don't stop on our account." The first guy said.

"Leave them be."

Si led me with one hand. "C'mon, let's get you home."

"Play safe boys!" I heard one of the guys say.

Further down the road, Si told me I was a fantastic kisser but I didn't know how to respond because I had never kissed anyone before. I thanked him, squeezed his hand and told him that he was the best kisser I had ever had. I wasn't lying.

We stopped in front of a beautiful square. There was a massive black iron fountain that reminded me of something that you would see in an old film when New York had horse drawn carriages and no electricity. A few birds were perched on the rim of the fountain singing. If this was where my day was going to end, I couldn't have thought of a better background. Si kissed me on the cheek.

"I wish I could stop time right now." He said.

"Me too."

He let go of my hand as we walked towards the subway. "It's not safe."

My feet landed firmly on the ground, the magic of the previous moment disappeared. The city had turned hard again. I knew he was right and I hated it.

He brushed against me as if by accident. "One day though."

"You think?"

"The world is changing Lu." He said those words like he had some inside knowledge. Like he was sure of it. I knew my world had changed that day. I took comfort in his words.

We sat on the train side by side up to Columbus Circle. Our legs pressed against each other in silence, the occasional glance to keep the connection. Si got off the train with me even though he didn't have too. I had to get the D train back to a worried mother and questions I had no answer for.

"See you Saturday?" He asked.

"Definitely!" My mind was already thinking of excuses to use to get back downtown. Spend the night at a friend's? Oh wait, no friends. School football game? Nope, she knew I hated sports. *I had to think of something.*

He hugged me and gave me a sly kiss on my neck which sent a sensation up and down my body. I tried hard to hide it. I walked away, leaving him waiting for the next train. Before climbing the stairs, I stopped and looked back. He smiled and winked. My heart skipped a few beats and I continued on my way.

When I got on the D train, I took my walkman out, placing the soft cushion earphones over my ears to drown out the sounds around me. I pressed play and "Heaven" by Bryan Adams started. It was strange that only the night before I had made that 80's mix tape when I should have been asleep. That I made it so the day wouldn't drag on as long as they usually did at school. It felt like another lifetime.

I watched the street numbers getting higher as the train sped up...*71st, 81st, 86th and so on*. I tried to fight off the loneliness that came over me as the train carried me home, away from Si, from my new friends and my new found freedom.

I exited Fordham station and walked down to the corner of Valentine Avenue. Looking up at the red brick building that was home, I dreaded walking up the five flights of stairs. When I reached the top, I took a deep breath and put my key in the door. As I turned the knob, I could hear her voice.

"*¿Mijo?*"

"Yea Ma, who else?"

She appeared in the hall as I closed the door behind me. She pointed her finger at me. "Don't get smart...*¿Adondes estabas?*"

35

"Library." The word slipped out without a thought. It was simple, easy and believable. *Library.* I had spent enough time hiding there from bullies. It would be a good place to spend more time at.

"Ah ok."

I walked over to her; her cheek was turned towards me expecting a kiss. "Sorry I'm late. I have a paper due Monday." *That was actually true.*

She scanned me up and down with her eyes. "Next time *llamame*, ok."

"Ok." I turned around and walked into my room, dropped my bag off on the floor near my bed and went back into the kitchen where she was dishing up dinner. Pepper steak with rice and beans.

I sat opposite her wishing it was Si in front of me and not her. She cut her steak into a few smaller pieces and took a bite, then looked at me. I looked down and cut my steak, taking a bite and remembering why this was my favorite meal, even if it had rice and beans; *as always.* The steak was tender and flavorful from the

36

copious amount of *adobo* and *sazón* she used. I smiled. *You couldn't beat her cooking.*

"I'm going to see *abuela* on Saturday. *¿Quieres venir?*"

Her question caught me off guard. I felt like one of those cartoon characters with a light bulb over his head. *Yes, an opportunity!* I downplayed my excitement. "I have that paper due, so if you don't mind."

She studied my composure or perhaps it was paranoia; guilt even. I continued eating, pushing the thought out of my head, afraid that she could see it written on my face.

"Ok, I'll leave you some *dinero para comer*, ok?"

"Thanks Ma."

I tried my best to behave like everything was the same but nothing was. The kid that left the house that morning did not come home that night. He never would again. I wondered if she had noticed the difference as her questions about my day were met with a simple *yes, no* and *okay.*

After dinner, I washed the dishes as she sat in the living room watching *Telemundo*. I excused myself to my bedroom faking tiredness but truth was I just wanted to be alone. I laid down on my bed staring up at the ceiling fan above me. As the blades turned, I thought more and more about Si's lips touching mine, his body pressed against mine. I could feel myself getting hard. I reached down in my pants and started to touch myself. Thinking about the heat from his breath and the things that we were yet to do, it didn't take long to find myself light headed and spinning with pleasure. It was the first time I had thought about someone I knew. I laid there until I heard footsteps. *Shit!* I grabbed the sheet and covered myself, taking off my shirt in the process so it looked like I was falling asleep. The door opened.

"You already in bed *mijo*?" Her tone was suspicious rather than questioning.

I faked a yawn. "Yea, ma."

"Ok." She walked over and kissed me on the forehead.

"Love you" I said.

"And you *mijo*. ¡*Siempre!*" The last word lingered in the room after she left the room.

I wiped off the mess I had made and turned towards the window. I wondered if Si was thinking of me at that very moment. I wondered if Cuchi and James really liked me. I drifted off hoping that sleep would make Saturday come quicker.

FRIDAY, JUNE 3, 1993

I stepped off the bus and there she was with her little gang of *guidettes,* Melanie *fucking* Sputano. She looked at me, smirked, turned towards her clones and said, "Did the air just get a little gayer."

They laughed. I was not in the mood.

"Fuck you Slutano!" I yelled back. *Silence.*

"What did you call me, fag?"

"Slutano. Shall I spell it for you?"

The sound of *oohs* and *ahhs* in the background. My heart was beating fast. I stood my ground staring right at her and trying not to give away how much I was shaking inside. I pictured Cuchi and James on either side of me for me strength. I could feel their approving looks, like two angel figures on each shoulder that had had enough of being nice.

She shook her head in defiance. "Wait til Anthony hears about this."

As I stood there, I knew it was going to be a long day if I stayed in school. She walked off, crew in tow. The sun was shining as it had been yesterday, another warm day in sight. I could hear the sound of the train pulling into the previous station. Decision time. Face Diagio or seize the day?

I ran up the stairs, pushing past a woman walking down who called me an "asshole." I pushed open the unsecured wooden exit only doors hearing the ticket booth lady yell, "Hey!" As I ran up to the platform, the train had just arrived. I got on, sat down and caught my breath. My thoughts drifted towards Si as I watched my school become further away as the train rolled on. I put my headphones on and pressed play on my walkman. My 80's tape was now playing Belinda Carlisle's "Heaven is a Place on Earth." For the first time, I felt like I knew what she was singing about.

41

Unlike yesterday I found myself on the train with a destination. I got off at Astor Place, walked down 8th Street. I smiled as I walked past *Patricia Fields*. The same girls were there, smoking like yesterday.

"Mothafucka had the nerve to stand ME up!"

"Oh HELLLLL no!"

"I packed up HIS shit and threw it in the trash for all the hood to see!"

"Mmmmhmmm...Where he belong gurl." They high fived each other.

They laughed; pleased with themselves. I crossed Sixth Avenue towards Christopher Street, heading towards *Oscar Wilde*, towards Si.

I opened the door and my heart sank. An older guy was behind the counter. He smiled and asked, "Can I help you honey?"

"Um, Is Si working today?"

He gave me a once over with his eyes, flashed a suspicious smile and responded, "Sorry honey, he's back next week."

"Oh okay."

"Do you want to leave a message?"

"No, it's okay. Seeing him tomorrow."

"Alright honey."

I left the shop feeling lost. Yesterday's high was replaced with disappointment. *What was I going to do now?* My stomach growled. I walked down past Sheridan Square, towards *Tiffany's*. I was hoping to run into Cuchi or James. I wanted the Village to feel like it had felt yesterday.

I sat in a booth next to the window even though I would be exposed to any cops walking past and ordered a coffee and a cheeseburger deluxe. I took in the faded decor of the diner. There was a mixture of waitresses with hardened expressions and people sitting in booths alone, like me. They sat in a world of their own, smoking cigarettes and reading copies of *The Post* and *The Daily News*. I took the book Si had given me out of my bag. Rubbed the cover of the smooth paperback, over the red lettering of "GAY" printed on the cover. It was the only thing I had that connected me to him. Touching it didn't make me feel so alone in this diner.

The waitress came back with a cup full of dark brown water that only passed for coffee the more half and half I put in. It didn't matter though, it was somewhere to sit and read my book.

I had read about ten pages and then my food arrived. I was interrupted by a knock on the window that made me smile.

"Ey *Papí*!" James said, his voice coming through the glass.

I waved him in. He came in and gave me a kiss on the cheek hello. My spirits lifted with the sight of him. Like a bit of yesterday had flowed into today.

"Bad little boy." He said. "Shouldn't you be in school?"

"Shouldn't you?"

"One day in the Village and you already trying to throw shade."

I smiled; feeling the color rise in my cheeks. I didn't quite understand what he meant but it was nice to feel a part of something. Something special. The manager came over to us. His expression was less than friendly.

"Let me guess, coffee?"

James rolled his eyes. "Billy, your diner would be empty if we didn't come in here. How much we spend here on any given Saturday?"

Billy looked at James up and down, and then me. "35 coffees with free refills do not pay my rent."

"That's an issue with your business model, not us." James said.

"Anything else?" A demand more than a question.

James looked at my food, then at Billy. Billy waited.

"And a complimentary water." James smiled as he said it.

Billy rolled his eyes and walked away. I tried not to giggle but it was useless. Billy returned within moments. He put the coffee and water down on the table with a force of resentment that made James say, "Oooh Mary."

"Where's Cuchi?"

"Oh she'll be down after school. You hanging out tonight?"

I shook my head. "Going out for dinner with my mom."

"That's sweet." He continued speaking as if he needed to get something off his chest. "My mama don't want anything to do with me. Not seen that heifer in a year." He said. There was a melancholy in his voice as if he had rehearsed that line in his mind enough to try and remove the sting of it.

"Oh, sorry."

James put some sugar in his coffee and stirred it. "Oh don't."

"What?" I didn't understand what had just happened.

"Look. My mama got issues but they hers not mine."

"Do you live with your dad?"

James pulled a cigarette out and offered me one. I declined out of fear of my mother smelling it on my breath but also I had no idea what to do with it. He lit it, exhaled and smiled.

"Live with my grandmother. Loves her little James. Says its God's place to judge, not hers."

The way he looked at me as he said it, made me smile.

"You not out to your mama?"

"Not even out to myself really."

He laughed. "One step at a time."

47

We talked about my date with Si. I told him about our walk, our talk. How we kissed in front of The Center. James listened but I couldn't help but feel like I sounded foolish. Like he had heard it before and was being polite.

"Si's, one of the good ones." He said as he put his cigarette out.

"Yea?"

"Yea, a lot of guys like Si but he's I don't know different, something about him?" James said. "It's like he knows what he's looking for." He shook his head. "Which let me tell you, most of the guys around here, don't."

"Do you like..?"

James shook his head. "Uh uh, far too *Wonder Bread* for me."

"*Wonder Bread?*"

"White boy. Gurl, we gotta educate you."

"Oh." I wondered what that made me but was afraid to ask.

James drank his coffee and when Billy came to refill it, he declined. I pushed my half eaten cheeseburger deluxe plate to one side. It looked better than it tasted.

"Let's take a walk." James said.

I asked for the bill and paid at the counter. We left the air conditioned comfort of *Tiffany's* and stepped back out into the humidity of the city.

"Where we going?" I asked.

"Just a little shop I love." James said with a smile on his face.

We turned the corner and walked down Christopher Street again. Like yesterday, it was busy with guys walking up and down the street. Some stopping to look at others, others turning around to be looked at. There was a playfulness that I enjoyed watching though I wasn't entirely sure what they were doing. A few looked at me and smiled, which made me blush. I walked close to James.

"You'll get used to the cruising?" He said.

I wasn't sure what he meant but I had showed enough innocence for one day. I nodded in agreement as if I certainly would.

We continued walking down, crossing Greenwich Avenue until we came to a shop called *Stick, Stone and Bone* that sold loads of New Age and Native American stuff. We walked in and a woman dressed in western, almost Native American style clothing walked around the counter and gave James a hug.

"Hey, this is Lu."

She looked at me as if she was studying me and then extended her hand to me. "Carol, pleasure to meet you."

There was music in the background that was relaxing and soothing although it had no lyrics, just sounds. The smell of incense took me back to my

Uncle Jose's house when he was trying to conceal the smell of pot. I walked further into the shop; boxes of incense, candles of all sizes and smells were scattered about as well as small baskets which held stones and descriptions of what they were for.

James walked past me. He picked up some rain scented candles, a book on Runes and a few stones. I don't know why it surprised me that he was buying these things as I knew very little about him, but it did. Like everything else that had happened in the last twenty four hours, I felt like I was in a different world.

I waited outside while he paid for his purchases. There was a feeling in the air that made me feel horny as I watched guys walk past in shorts, some in tank tops, a few shirtless enjoying another hot day in the city. I wish Si had been working or I knew where he would be.

"Bye Carol." James said as he came outside and then turned to me.

I wanted to ask him about his beliefs but didn't know how to so I suggested we walk down to the pier but he wanted to head east because he was meeting Cuchi near *Patricia Field's* later.

We headed towards Washington Square Park. The streets were so alive for the daytime and I dreaded having to travel back to The Bronx. I wished I didn't have to travel back ever. I wanted to hang out and belong somewhere like all kids my age wanted to do.

At home, I hung out with myself in the four corners of my gray colored bedroom that was plastered with posters from *Teen Beat* and *BOP* with 80's singers like Belinda Carlisle, Tiffany and bare-chested rockers like Sebastian Bach whose looks I loved more than his music. An easy way of having some eye candy on the wall without my mom questioning it although I think Uncle Jose knew. He used to smile when he saw the posters and shake his head like he understood.

I wanted to stay down here with all the hot guys who walked around not hiding who they were.

"You think a lot?" James said; snapping me out of my thoughts.

"Huh, guess so. Not used to talking to other people."

"I'm like that at school."

I stopped in my tracks. "Really?"

We were stood outside *The Pink Pussycat.* James reached for a cigarette out of his bag. "Survival baby, survival." He lit his cigarette.

"I just thought." But I didn't know how to finish what I wanted to say.

"School is school but here," he put his arms out as if everything was his and his alone. "This is real life, our real life. You'll figure it out." He took a drag and exhaled.

It was the first time I wanted a cigarette but the mental image of my mother's disapproving face stopped me from asking for one. I knew what he was saying but I didn't want to have to live like that. I wanted it to feel like this everywhere. To feel like I could be myself. Only twenty four hours had passed since I found other people like me; I was hooked.

In the end, all I could say was "hope so."

We reached the park which was lively with chess players, musicians, students sitting on the grass, indifferent police officers, men hurrying in and out of the public toilets and people rollerblading. We headed for the fountain and sat on the edge. James reached into his bag of purchases and produced a dark but sort of metallic stone.

"Here. For you." He said all smiles.

"What is it?"

"Hematite. It helps absorb negative energy. Clears the way for good things."

The stone was smooth and had a beautiful shine in the sun. I was touched and unsure what to do with it.

"Baby, keep it in your pocket and it will do the trick but wash it first under water and hold it in your hand. Think good things."

"Why?"

James could have been annoyed by my questions but the look in his eyes was tender and sympathetic. He looked eager to educate me on this. "It'll transfer your energy to the stone."

"Oh okay." It still made no sense to me but I decided it didn't have too.

I put the stone in my pocket and thanked him. We sat there watching the world go by. The park felt like the center of the world. All types crossing paths in this concrete square with spots of green on either side, dominated by an arch that looked as if it gave birth to the road in front of it. We hung out and watched the world go by until it was time for me to head home and have my obligatory Friday night dinner with my mom. Tomorrow I would be back. Tomorrow I would see Si and that thought made the subway ride home okay.

Mom was putting her earrings on in the hallway mirror when I got home. She smiled and then turned to face me. "How do I look?"

"Good. Beautiful." That she did. She was wearing a black vest like top, flair bottom black pants and her black sandals. Her hair was held in place with hairspray, freshly dyed that blue black color she loved.

She walked over to me, gave me a kiss and said "I put clothes out on the bed for you. Go change."

"Where we going?"

"Out. I thought it would be fun."

"Okay." I said. I walked into my bedroom and saw the creased jeans on the bed with a starched white shirt next to them. We now had very different definitions of fun.

Mom was in the kitchen having a small glass of wine when I finished changing. She took one look at me and said "*Mijo*, you look more like your father every day." My dad was hit by a car when I was three years old. I could count everything I knew about him on one hand: His name was Carlos, his nickname was "Loco," he was a mechanic, he played guitar, and apparently I looked like him.

"Thanks."

She drank the rest of her wine, grabbed her keys and purse and we left the apartment. The corridor was buzzing with the sounds of other families starting their weekend. The smell of rice and beans, cooked meats marinated in *adobo* and the brass sounds of salsa music created a festive air to the otherwise dull grey walls of our Pre-war building; a building with broken moulds, stark light bulbs and painted over murals that once spoke of prosperity to middle class white families.

It was one of those nights where the humidity had risen which sent my mother into immediate meltdown. "Ay, *mijo, este calor.* This is why I can't live in Puerto Rico." For an islander, she detested the heat. Mom was happiest in her winter coat with the fur around the collar, her leather gloves and warm pants. She took my arm so I could lead her as we walked past people. She was nodding and smiling like she was showing me off and I think she was. She loved to tell the neighbors about my grades and how well I was doing in school. I smiled but it was forced. I felt like a phony. I doubt she would be proud of my behaivor the last two days. I wanted to be downtown with the rest of the misfits.

"Where we going?"

"*El Chino.*"

We turned right at the corner and walked towards the Grand Concourse, crossing the massive boulevard in two stages and up the street to *El Chino* as my mother called it. The restaurant was called *El Morro de China* and run by Hector Chan; a friend of our family who grew up with my mother and uncle in Aguadilla. He was a Chinese Puerto Rican who could flip between Cantonese and Spanish as if he were turning a page in a book. Had it not been for him, I would never have passed my written Spanish finals last year, since my mother's patience had worn thin with correcting my essays and grammar.

Hector was at the door speaking with the hostess when we walked in.

"Maria, *mi amor*!" He said. His arms stretched out wide.

My mother walked into them, hugging him back and giving him two kisses.

Hector then held his hand out to me, as I went to shake it; he pulled me into his arms. "*Luis, te pareces mas como tu padre...pero tambien veo un pocito de Jose, no?*"

His comparison to my Uncle made me nervous. My mother looked at me and dismissed it. "*Bueno, un pocito pero mas como Carlos.*"

Hector showed us to our table which was in a bamboo covered booth towards the massive mural of *El Morro* in San Juan. The restaurant decor was over the top. There were individual bamboo huts as booths on either side of the mural. A fountain in the center like the ones you find in the courtyards of Spanish homes and smaller tables around it. The music alternated between traditional Chinese music and

Felipe Rodriguez *boleros*; my mother's favorite singer.
The food was good and mom loved Hector, so it was
one of our haunts. Apart from her own, Hector's
cooking was about the only other thing she enjoyed
eating.

Mom ordered herself a Piña Colada and a Coke for
me. She went to look at the menu which made me
smile as she was a creature of habit.

"Don't give me that look."

"You always order the same thing Ma."

"Oh yea, you so smart what am I going to have."

"Hot and sour soup, an egg roll, beef with broccoli
and shrimp fried rice."

She put the menu down. Looked at me as if she was
searching for a sign and said, "I should have never
taught you how to speak."

"Told you."

The waitress returned with our drinks and we ordered our food. I ordered the same thing as mom with the exception of shrimp fried rice, opting for the pork instead. We were both creatures of habit.

She took a sip of her drink and then said, "You don't look like Jose, *pero* I see him in you."

My body temperature started to rise and my head filled with paranoid questions of *what does that mean? What does she mean? Does she know something? Does it show in my face? She must know something.* "Really?" Was all I could say in response.

She shook her head. "He was quiet too *cuando era* your age. Used to read a lot. Didn't fit in with the other boys." There was a sadness in the tone of her voice as she spoke.

I reached over the table and squeezed her hand which snapped her out of it. Her eyes glistened with a small layer of tears forming. She patted them dry and as if the moment had never happened, returned to the present.

61

"I miss him too."

"*Abuela* still doesn't mention him." She said.

"She's a bitch, that's why." I said; a comment that was met with a slap on the wrist.

"¡*Respeto!* I didn't raise you like that."

I recoiled from the sting of her slap and thought about the mood that had set in. I hated seeing her so sad. "At least he had us." I said.

"Well that bitch wasn't there was she?" She smiled and took a big sip of her drink.

We both laughed. I knew that my mother had a duty to *Abuela* but that it went no further than that. I think that is why she never pressured me to go along for a visit.

The food came and she ordered another drink. We spoke around topics, like her job and how she hated her co-worker Beatrice who always criticised the way she filed the patient folders. I told her about school but not about the bullying. As we talked and laughed, a sense of peace came over me; one of belonging. I thought about what it would be like if Si, Cuchi and James were here with us. If these moments were all that I had, then I could say I was happy. For once in my life, nothing but good things were in it. It was a shame that they were not all connected.

Hector waved us off as we left the restaurant and stepped back into the muggy night. The streets were loud with traffic, music and drunken people. My mother was a little tipsy and used me for support. It was just her and I now; and I wished I could tell her the truth about my week, but I was afraid. I was afraid that the kind of night we were sharing would never happen again.

When we got home, she kissed me on the forehead and said, "*Tu Padre* would be proud of you." She was a bit unsteady so I walked her to her bedroom. I turned on the light for her and she sat on the bed looking like she was trying to plan her next move.

"I wish my brother was still alive." She said as she looked down at the floor. She then looked at me. "I bet you two would have a lot to talk about."

I tried to hide the panic that was setting in. *What did she mean by that? Did she know about me? How?*

I walked over to her and sat next to her. I put m arm around her. "We talk Ma."

She put her head on my shoulder. "I know *mijo*." She then sat up and shook her head. "Those Piña Colada's were *fuerte, no?*"

I laughed it off and got up from the bed. "You need help getting to bed?"

"No *mijo*. I'll be fine."

"Okay Ma. I love you." I walked towards the bedroom door.

"*Mijo?*"

I turned around.

"It doesn't bother me that people think you're a bit like Jose." She smiled. "He was a good man."

"He was." I said. "Good night Ma."

"*Buenas Noche mijo.*"

I left her bedroom and took a deep breath before walking to my room.

I laid down on the bed after undressing. I watched the blades of the ceiling fan go round and round as if it were a stopwatch counting down the hours till I saw Si again. Till I was able to be myself again.

SATURDAY JUNE 5, 1993

I was doing my best *nonchalant nothing to see here* look as I watched my mother get ready to leave the house. I was still in my boxers and t-shirt for authenticity purposes and had not showered yet. No way she would think I was going downtown.

"*Mijo*, Hector does the best *comida China*, no?" She said as she put her keys and wallet in her black purse; the one I bought last year for her birthday after she complained she did not have a decent bag. I used some of the money that Uncle Jose had left me when he died. He would have appreciated what I bought. It was the first time I had taken the subway downtown on my own and she was upset that I had not told her but I think the fact the purse came from *Bloomingdales* smoothed over that fact.

"Yea, it was nice to go out."

She brushed her hair back with her hand, zipped up her purse and then came towards me. "*Te deje $20 en la cocina*, ok?" She gave me a kiss on the cheek. "*Dios de bendiga.*" With that, she was gone.

I stood there composing myself, exhaling with relief that I managed not to raise any suspicions. I walked back into my bedroom to lay out my outfit. It was boiling in the room so I opened the window. I wasn't fond of my own chicken legs but it was too hot for jeans. I cut a pair of jeans that I had become too big for into shorts. I rolled the jagged bits up to make a cuff that fell just above my knee. I decided on the first shirt I ever picked out myself after finally defeating my mother in the clothes buying war. It was a green and blue horizontal striped t-shirt from the *GAP*; a store my mother saw as a rip off when she could buy me three shirts at *Youngworld* for that price. I finished the outfit with the *Payless* equivalent of black *Keds*. I smiled at how cute it looked.

I turned the radio on; Duran Duran's "Say A Prayer" was playing on *Z100*. I stripped off and went

to shower. The water provided a relief from the heat
and as I dried off, I could feel myself starting to sweat.
When I returned to the bedroom, Roxette's "Almost
Unreal" was playing on the radio and I took that as a
good sign of the day ahead of me. I removed the towel
from my waist and dried my back as I pulled it left to
right; singing along to the music.

After getting dressed and giving myself a thumbs up
in the mirror, I packed my bag with the usual stuff
(minus my school books): black and white marble
composition book that was my journal. A couple of
mix tapes for my walkman, *Reflections of a Rock Lobster*,
my walkman, headphones, spare batteries, and the $10
emergency money I kept in the lining of my glasses
case. I put the hematite James had given me in the
little pocket above the bigger one on the right side of
my jean shorts, the one no one knew what to do with.
Or at least I didn't know what it was for.

I looked at my alarm clock on my night stand. It
was approaching 12. I knew if I left now then I would

be able to walk from W4th Street, back up to *The Center.*

There was a line of people waiting to buy tickets at Fordham Road. I could hear the train coming so I made the decision to hop the train as the attendant argued with a customer over something. I quickly opened the wooden gates and ran down the stairs, jumping into the carriage as the doors opened. I sat in one of the forward facing seats, reached into my bag for my walkman, put my headphones on and lost myself in "Kids in America."

The sun was beating down as I exited W4th Street Station and walked north up to Greenwich past the *Pizzeria Uno* at the top of Christopher Street. I turned right and headed towards 7th Avenue. I thought about Uncle Jose as I walked past *Uncle Charlie's.* It was another name that I remember him saying when he would tell my mother about nights out. It was weird that being in the Village made me remember more about him. It felt like he was closer to me than he had ever been. I looked up as if he could hear me and whispered, "I wish you were here." A pigeon flew by low as if it were a sign.

As I approached St Vincent's Hospital, a sudden feeling of anxiety hit me. *What if Si wasn't there? What if Cuchi and James weren't there? What would these other people think of me? What would they look like? Would they laugh at me?* A panic like the first day of a new school set in. I stopped myself on the corner of 12th Street and composed myself. I took some deep breathes and then long exhales. I started to repeat to myself, "I belong here, calm down."

I looked around and a diner across the street caught my attention; *The Village Star.* Just under the awning I saw Si holding one of those blue and white coffee cups with the Greek columns. He was wearing baggy brown shorts, a plain white t-shirt, green converse high tops and his sunglasses above his forehead which held his dirty blond bangs up. He crossed the street, looking both ways with a confidence that made him look sexy. I called out to him when he reached my side of the street.

One flash of his acknowledging smile and my anxiety ceased on the spot. I walked towards him, not wanting to break contact; feeling each long step as I approached him. He put one arm around me when I got to him. I could feel the dampness of his t-shirt from the sweat and the scent of *Farenheit* on his neck as he pulled me close. I recognized the scent because when I bought my mother's purse a very cute cologne guy gave me two samples of it and winked at me. I rarely used it myself because it was so expensive and I never had a reason to wear it. The top of my head touched that space where his neck and shoulder met.

"Now my day is perfect." He said and kissed my forehead. I looked up at him, our lips met in that way that made them glide and caused me to get excited. He squeezed me tight.

"Good to see you again." I pulled away so we could walk and he gripped my hand; leading me. We turned the corner and I could see a crowd of teenagers standing outside as if they were a mob. It really did feel like the first day at school but as long as he kept holding my hand, I felt safe.

As we approached, a large girl in flannel, jean shorts and black boots turned towards us and said, "Si, you always get first dibs on new meat, don't you."

He snapped his fingers, "you know it." I looked around for Cuchi and James but they were nowhere to be seen.

Si then walked towards her and gave her a big hug; she lifted him off the ground and shook him side to side.

He then introduced us. Casey wrapped her arms around me as a mother would a child; I was being crushed between her big chest and arms. "Hello, baby, sorry about the tease. Just how we are around here."

I caught Si's eye and he winked at me which made me feel comfortable. Casey released me and she and Si introduced me to the group. Everyone seemed nice and it felt like I had their approval because I was with Si.

We were about to walk into *The Center* when Cuchi and James were walking out. Cuchi was in a red dress, black high heels, and a blonde wig which against her mocha skin reminded me of the Puerto Rican women in my block with bad bleach jobs.

"Wrong way ladies." Casey said.

"That's just perspective." Cuchi pushed past Casey; James followed.

"I wondered where you two were?" I said.

James gave me and Si a kiss on the cheeks. "Oh that took time." He said, pointing at Cuchi.

Cuchi shot us all a nasty look and pulled out a cigarette.

We waited with Cuchi as she smoked. The rest of the group made their way towards some double doors that led into the courtyard. We followed them after Cuchi put her cigarette out and fluffed up her hair as she prepared for her entrance.

The two guys from the other day were there and gave Si and I a smile, then took one another's hands. We then passed through another set of doors into an annex. The room was large with a makeshift stage towards the front. There were a handful of people standing while the rest of the group took seats. A large circle of about 30 chairs were being filled by teens of both genders and some in between. It was what I had wished my high school looked like: preppy guys, thug looking guys and girls, a few girls that looked like cheerleaders, effeminate guys, some butch girls, a couple of guys who looked like they could be on the football team. It was a mix I had not expected and one that made me wonder what I must look like to them.

A matron like black woman with dreads called us all to attention. She had a smile that reminded me of Whoopi Goldberg and her voice was calming. She introduced herself as Eunice and then turned to the five people around her. They introduced themselves as Bill, Terry, Spike, Nate and Mary; they were on the leadership council and alongside Eunice, headed the group. It was all very student council but kind of nice too.

After they introduced themselves, it was the groups turn. Each person in the room spoke with a confidence that made my anxiety hit the roof. The words, "Gay," "Lesbian," "Bi" said with a pride that took me by surprise. The support from the group shown with claps and smiles.

It came to my turn and as much as I wanted to grab Si's hand, I couldn't. I was paralysed and all eyes were on me. I looked around. The anticipation on everyone's face made my stomach growl aloud with nerves. I caught Si's face through the corner of my eye. He was smiling in a supportive way and he patted my knee as if to say, "its ok." I then looked at Eunice; her smile coaxed the words right out of my mouth.

"Hi...um...I'm Luis...or Lu, both are fine." I took a deep breath. "Um...first time here."For some reason, I raised my hand. I put my hand down and noticed a few people smile as if they were holding back laughter but that could have just been how I saw it. I looked around the room; my face felt like it was burning up. I took another deep breath. "I guess, I'm...well, no, I am...I'm gay." There was a round of applause and a few people in the room said hello back with a mixture of *Luis* and *Lu*. The words out loud opened a floodgate in my body. The tension went from my shoulders down to my feet like water going down a drain. I felt unsteady.

Eunice said "Thank you and Welcome." It was now Si's turn. He gripped my hand and held it as he introduced himself to the group.

The meeting continued with more introductions and then an exercise in which we were split into two groups. One group had to pretend to be homophobic and calling the other group terrible names, then the groups switched. The purpose was to see how those words affected us but also to reclaim the language and make those words positive. To see them as part of a rich identity which we were all a part of. I didn't quite get it all but I knew that it was important. After the session we all had to hug each other and apologize for the hurt those words caused. It was part of healing I guess. I had been called those names at school for such a long time and they still hurt, no matter how much time had passed or what I told myself.

When the meeting ended, the group was outside *The Center*, making noise and standing around with no sign of moving in any direction. It felt amazing. This was like after school but with people like me. I listened to the bits of conversation as if they were loose flower petals in the wind. "*Gurl, I ain't go no money for the diner....Let's just go to the Pier....ay, it's hot....oooh you got pot?....I need food.*"

"You hungry?" Si asked, breaking me out of my trance.

I shook my head. "Not really."

"Do you want to walk down to the Pier?"

"Yea." I really wanted to experience walking down Christopher Street again. I wanted to be seen hand in hand with Si; to feel like I was the luckiest guy in the world.

Si called out to Cuchi and James to let them know we were heading away from The Center. Cuchi nodded her head in a desperate *yes* manner. James was already walking ahead. The four of us walked on as the group continued their indecisiveness.

"It's like a dysfunctional amoeba sometimes." Si said to me.

I chuckled. As we walked away I heard a deep feminine voice reprimand the group. "Children, I may be a woman but I can assure you I have no maternal bone in my body. Move along quietly please."

"Uh oh, they gone pissed off Roberta." James said through giggles.

"Roberta?" I asked.

"She works front desk." James said.

"I love huh." Cuchi added, "Don't get on huh nerves though."

"Okaaaaay" Si snapped his fingers. The three of them laughed. I played along, unsure of what was so funny. *Guess you had to know Roberta.*

As we turned the corner and walked down towards Christopher Street I could hear the noise of the rest of the group getting closer. Some had splintered off towards *Tiffany's*. There was a loud wedding party coming out of a church.

"Never gets old." James said in a tone that made me think it did.

"What?" I asked.

"*Tony n' Tina's Wedding*. It's a show."

"Oh it's not real?"

"Nope."

We held back and Si suggested we go into a shop called *The Loft* which was stocked with underwear, bathing suits that looked impractical and a lot of rainbow colored merchandise.

The sales guy rushed over to Si. "*Mi amor*, how are you?"

Si kept my hand held. "I'm good baby, you?"

He threw his hands in the air. "You know, *asi asi*, and who's this?" His eyes scanned me as if I were a cake in a glass container.

Si reeled me in closer to him. "Lu." He then looked at me and smiled. "My new boyfriend, I think."

The word "boyfriend" floated in the air like a feather blowing in the wind. The most beautiful feather caught in a summer breeze with the gentle sun behind it. I blushed with a mixture of happiness and embarrassment.

"Ay, *que lindo*, you two." His Spanglish made me feel very much at home, memories of Uncle Jose resurfaced, as if he were guiding me today. He introduced himself as Arturo. He seemed like the kind of guy Uncle Jose would know.

I walked over to the counter, leaving them to continue talking and saw some rainbow rings on a chain. I remembered that Uncle Jose had some he kept next to his military dog tags. Mom said he had been forced to leave the Air Force because of who he was. It was the reason mom cared for him out of her own pocket in his last days because the government would not. I wanted the rings myself as a connection to him.

"How much are these?" I asked, interrupting their conversation.

"The freedom rings, *Papi*?"

"Yes." Freedom rings, the very sound of the words summed up how I was feeling at the moment. How I had been feeling since I met Si, Cuchi, and James; since I discovered the village.

Arturo waved his hand. "Ay, take them. Just put some money in the collection box, ok." I put $5 in a container with a red ribbon on it, for Uncle Jose. I could feel his approval. Si walked over to me and pulled out a chain from under his shirt that I had not noticed.

"Guess we match now." He kissed me on the lips. Our moment interrupted by Arturo.

"Ay, ok, enough. You are too cute."

He made kissing motions at us as we walked outside to continue down Christopher Street with James and Cuchi who were fixing themselves in a big mirror that was outside the shop.

I caught a glimpse of what Si and I looked like as a couple. He was taller than me and had a glow to him, like it was something magical. I was awkward looking but there was a twinkle in my eyes that I had not seen before and I could see life pulsing through my veins.

We continued onward to the Pier with a confidence as if we owned the sidewalk and everyone else was just renting it. Cuchi strutting her stuff in heels. James walked as if he was on a stage for the entire world to see and then there was us, holding hands; not caring whose eyes were upon us.

Just before crossing the West Side Highway I saw some pink triangles spray painted on the sidewalk.

"Do those mark the gay blocks?" I asked.

James jumped into answer. "No baby, those mark where some ignorant motherfucker attacked one of us."

"A reminder of how far we have to go." Si squeezed my hand.

"And fight." Cuchi continued.

"Don't worry, nothing gonna happen to you while we around." James said to me. There was an assurance in his voice that made me feel safe. I was beginning to see how James had that affect on me. We all held hands as we crossed the West Side Highway. The group of loud kids from the other day were there with a boom box; dancing as if everyone was watching to see the stars they knew they were. Not a single apology for the scene they were creating.

"They always here?" I asked.

"Here is the only place some of them have." Si said.

It felt like *here* was not just theirs but ours; mine even. The Pier was busier than it was on weekdays. There was a mixture of shirtless guys on roller blades, couples walking hand in hand, girls kissing girls, and us. The haze from the humidity was so thick, the end of the Pier seemed like a mirage and New Jersey was barely visible. We continued walking to the end much to Cuchi's protest about having to climb over the barrier in heels. Si held her hand as she stepped through the hole in the fence. Her beauty in the derelict surroundings made me wish I had had a camera.

Cuchi sat down on a raised bit of wood which provided the only real elevation. The end of the pier had some large holes where you could see the river below and although it looked dangerous, it felt like the safest place in the world. The city skyline was behind us, the murky waters of the Hudson flowed under us as cruise ships and the *Circle Line* floated past. Some of the group were sitting at the very end of the Pier with their feet dangling; passing a joint.

The joint eventually made its way to us and I took a little bit. I had never just hung out before but that was all it was. Si kept putting his arms around me. Every time his skin touched mine I could feel myself getting higher and higher. We were all just teens, doing stupid teen things like getting high, making fun of each other, laughing. We stayed there till near sundown when the orange colors appeared over New Jersey. The heat had still not let up and as others decided where to go next, I kissed Si's neck, tasting his salty skin as he sank into my arms. I didn't even know why I did it or how I knew what to do but it felt right. It felt like the most natural thing in the world. We sat there listening to the mixture of voices, the hum of the city and river smacking against the pier supports. *Life was perfect.*

I could feel Si's stomach growl. "Hungry?"

"A little, you?"

"Yea."

We stood up. Everyone else had gone apart from the four of us. James and Cuchi were passing a cigarette between them and had one ear phone each singing along to "Damn, Wish I Was Your Lover" by Sophie B Hawkins.

"*Tiffany's*?" Si asked them.

Cuchi and James shook their heads along to the music and we all walked back towards the West Side Highway. The boom box was still blaring and there were more kids than before, dancing, laughing and calling each other out in insults.

We had just made it across the street to the corner of Christopher when I heard someone yell out "Fucking Faggots!"

Cuchi yelled back. "And?" James added a snap of the fingers. Their responses flowed as natural as someone saying excuse me.

The car stopped and a voice said, "What the fuck did you say?" There was something familiar in the way he said "fuck."

I turned around to look and I felt the color drain from my face. *Fuck!*

"Look who we have here. Told you he was fag, Mel."

I could see the top of her hair, the shine of a half of bottle of *Rave* holding her rat nest up. Melanie *fucking* Sputano.

The four of us and the two of them were separated by less than a couple of feet. Anthony and Melanie were shaking their heads; an evil in their eyes told me "everyone is going to know come Monday."

"You know these idiots?" Si asked.

"They go to my school." I had forgotten that Diagio had passed his driving test but then again he had been left back a year too.

Cuchi took one step closer to the car. The sound of her heel on the street, tapped as if to say, "come on, try it *cabron*!"

Anthony defiant as usual. Sat in his car, engine off. "Fucking disgusting AIDS faggots."

Cuchi took another step towards the car and said, "oh and you such a man. Step out the fucking car and say it to my face!"

I could hear Mel say, "Just leave it Anthony."

He turned towards her. "Fuck you. I'm not letting some faggot talk to me like that." His manners never failed to make me question what it was about him that made girls swoon.

He opened the car door, slammed it and stepped towards Cuchi; who stood there with no fear in her eyes. Not even a flinch. He went to put his hand in her face and she grabbed him by the balls, digging her nails as she twisted. Anthony screamed like a baby and I smiled as I heard him make the noises I would make when he pinned me down on the floor and punched me in the ribs. Cuchi then grabbed him by the throat and pushed him against the car. Melanie got out of the car but was stopped in her tracks by James who said, "Bitch, get back in the car."

I had never seen such a look of terror in Melanie's face and watching Anthony disarmed against the car gave me a sense of justice I had never felt before. All the beatings he had given me had lead him to this point. His downfall at the hands of a six foot drag queen.

"Say sorry!"

"Owww."

"Say it!" Cuchi had loosened her grip on his throat but not his balls. She had her heel pressed on his foot too.

"Fuck you!" There was less fire in his response. The words forced rather than meant.

Another twist.

"Owwwww..Fuck!"

"Sorry honey, the men I go for scream like little bitches in the bedroom not the streets."

"Owww..I'm...I'm"

"You're what?"

"I'm sorry." The apology forced out of pain. I went to walk towards them but Si held me back.

"That's right you are! Now let me explain something you little piece of shit. If you lay a hand or even think about touching my boy over there I will show up and wait for you, dressed in my highest heels and beat your homophobic hateful ass in front of all your posse and then the following day I will show up with my girlfriends and beat your ass again. *¿Comprende cabron?*"

Anthony looked stunned and what had been satisfying had now become uncomfortable to watch.

"Now get back in your piece of shit *guido* mobile and get the fuck out of here!"

Cuchi released Anthony and took a step back. Anthony stood there catching his breath as if he was trying to get the energy to say something back.

"Get the fuck out of here!" Cuchi said again; a command more than a request. She then yelled out across the street. "Tisha! Wanda!"

I looked over and saw the drag queens I kept walking past outside of *Patricia Fields*. One of them yelled back. "Hey Cuchi! What's up baby?"

Cuchi pointed at Anthony. "We got a basher here."

Anthony rushed to get back into the car when he saw the two towering figures approaching his car. One of them threw a bottle at the car, smashing it against the side Melanie was sitting on. She screamed as if she was being chased in a horror film.

Si put his arms around me and my weight fell against his body. "You okay?"

I wasn't but I knew I would be. Cuchi came over to me and put her arms around me too. "He won't bother you again." James was lost in the spectacle of Wanda and Tisha chasing Anthony's IROC-Z around the corner. Cuchi snapped him out of it and we continued walking up towards *Tiffany's*.

"The ugly side of being gay." Si said.

"I thought that was Cuchi with no makeup?" James said, breaking the tension and silence that had encircled us.

"¡*Cabron*!" Cuchi slapped James against the arm.

We all laughed and when I thought about it more, I couldn't help let out a laugh louder than the rest. When they had stopped, I continued laughing driven by freedom and anxiety. Tears started to come out but I didn't know if they came from pain or joy. Cuchi once again put her arms around me, cradling me almost. "I know baby." I looked at Si and a flash of his eyes calmed me again.

When we got to *Tiffany's,* James said to all of us, "I need to call *Limelight.* Four tonight?"

Si explained it was a club in an old church and that they had a connection that could put us on the guest list. Without a second thought I answered, "Yes."

That morning goodbye kiss from my mother seemed like a lifetime ago. My life in The Bronx was a million miles away and down here time and the world felt like it had infinite possibilities. Here, I could live in the moment. James excused himself to make the call from the payphone in the diner.

Cuchi let out a squeal which got the waiter's attention.

"I told you no scenes in here."

Cuchi waved him off. "Billy, all you have is scenes here. Look around."

He shook his head in annoyance. "Been trying to get into my ass since the first moment he looked at me." Cuchi continued, which made both Si and I shake our heads in unison.

We had a few more hours to kill before going to the club so we sat and drank coffee till we couldn't drink anymore, then walked around the backstreets of the Village, sitting on stoops and passing joints until the residents yelled at us for making noise. We walked

93

towards 7th Avenue and stopped off at *Two Boots* for some munchie food. We walked with our slices. When we got to the corner of 13th and 7th Ave, Si insisted we walked down the tree lined street. As James and Cuchi walked in front of us, we stopped when we got to an old church.

"This is where I want to live someday." Si said to me. I remembered his promise to show me something on that street. There it was, a converted church. Through the side entrances you could see the windows and doors which led to the units. I saw two guys curled up on a sofa, the glow of the television illuminating them. One gently squeezed the other. I put my arm around Si and thought of the possibility of us one day, doing just that. Maybe even there.

"It's so cool." The words left my mouth in that slow stoned sounding voice. We were interrupted by Cuchi's voice.

"Bitches, c'mon!"

I looked at this amazing building once more, taking in the columns, the potted plants and a sign that read Presbyterian Church. I took Si's hand and we walked on, catching up with Cuchi and James.

When we arrived at the club, the line was around the corner but James led us to the front which was cordoned off by a velvet rope. There was a slim guy with green hair, glitter on his face, lipstick and platform boots which made him look over seven feet tall. He greeted James with a scream and a kiss. I held back, unsure if I was going to be let in. He lifted the rope, gave me a wink and a smile which I took as reassurance. Si took my hand from the front. I could feel the eyes of the people on line, like daggers being thrown across the room. In that moment, I felt like I was famous. I was no longer invisible.

No questions asked; I found myself inside the church with lights, lasers and hanging cages with dancers in them. I had never heard this thumping music but it was infectious. Each beat seemed to control the lights and the beams shooting across the vaulted ceilings. All around us were people dressed in multi colored outfits, others shirtless and sweaty. Many of them with their eyes glazed over in a look of euphoria. I thought back to that time my mom took me to *Ringling Bros.* I was in awe.

"They're on E." Si said as if he knew what question was on the tip of my tongue.

"What's that?"

He pulled me in front of him by the waist. I could feel his hips swaying behind me as he whispered into my ear, "something that's not for tonight." He then kissed me on the neck as his hand took a hold of mine.

We walked up to the balcony overlooking the dance floor which gave us a view of the club to see if we could find Cuchi and James who had walked off ahead of us into the crowd when we came in. There was a guy that stood next to us who was dressed as if he didn't want to be there; as if he should be in an office. He was smoking a joint until something caught his eye. He tapped Si on the arm and offered him the joint. Si took a hit, and then passed it to me. I inhaled a tiny amount already feeling higher than I ever thought possible. I passed it back to the guy as another cute guy wrapped his arms around him; he seemed surprised by it but he didn't fight it.

Si pointed down to the dance floor where Cuchi and James had found a spot as near center as they could, hands in the air and commanding the attention around them. I thought I saw Cuchi smile and wink but it could have been the lights. We walked back down and made our way through the crowds to them. I didn't know I could dance, or even sure that I was dancing but none of it mattered with Si's arms around me.

When I noticed the time, it was about 3am; which should have meant more to me than it did but we continued dancing for about another hour and although I should have been worried, I wasn't. When we left the club, the city air was cool. It was a nice break from the fog and heat of the club. Cuchi staggered towards us, put her arms around me, and whispered something inaudible in my ears as James mimed a pill taking action.

"You want some help?" Si asked James.

"Nah baby, you two deserve a little alone time."

Si hailed a taxi for them and helped them in. He then turned to me; put his hands in his pocket a little unsure. "So you want to head back to my place?"

"Where else would we go?" I smiled. He came towards me and put his arms around my waist.

"Ever walk through the city this time in night, or morning I guess."

I shook my head. "I've never stayed up this late."

"You're in for treat." Si said. "This is the best time to see the city."

He had a look in his eye like he had waited to share this secret of the city in the early hours of the morning. I wanted to hold his hand but held back because we were walking away from the club, away from the safety of our fellow misfits. Instead, I bumped into him and smiled. He bumped me back and we continued walking Uptown on 6th Avenue.

I thought about my mother for a brief moment as we took a turn towards Broadway after Herald Square.

I told Si about the weird conversation my mother and I had after our dinner.

"Mother's have a weird way of sensing things." He said.

"Did yours?" I asked.

He laughed. "She always says I had an unhealthy obsession with Belinda Carlisle."

"I guess we both do then." I responded. Music seemed to be something else we had in common.

Times Square was peaceful, as if the city that never sleeps was taking a nap. I thought about Uncle Jose as we passed the Howard Johnson's. He had taken me there once when I was younger. I couldn't remember why we were downtown but I remember the grilled ham and cheese sandwich.

"That's my comfort food." Si said. "With *Campbell's* tomato soup."

"Wow. That's what my mom makes for me when I'm sick"

"Must be a mom thing." He said. "My dad does most of the cooking though but my mom can heat up things like nobody's business." He laughed at his own private joke.

I told him about Uncle Jose and how much I missed him. Maybe it was my own coming out or that my mother was right, I wished he had still been alive so I could talk to him, or maybe it was that I wanted to share everything with Si. As I talked about him, I felt freer. I was getting space in my head which was making me think clearer.

Si listened to me talk and at times it looked like he wanted to put his arms around me and tell me it would all be okay but it wasn't safe. Instead, we bumped against one another as if that was only contact we were allowed to have. To the outside world, it probably looked like we were tired or high. Each bump was a kiss we could share without fear.

We continued on Broadway towards *Lincoln Center* and then onto Columbus Avenue. I asked Si how many boyfriends he had had which made him laugh.

"How many do you think I have had?"

"A few?" I said.

He shook his head. "Just one in high school. Not really worth mentioning it."

I had a feeling he didn't want to talk anymore about it and I didn't want to ruin the magic of our walk.

"You might be my first." I said.

"I wonder how I can turn that *might* into a definite." He responded and bumped into me again.

We turned on the corner of W 78th Street and Columbus. The street was lined with large trees, big houses with large windows that jutted out of them and imposing stoops that were grander than the ones in the Village.

We stopped in front of one and entered through the basement, into a large kitchen that looked more like it belonged in the country than in the city. It was like that show *Kate and Allie*.

"Wow, this is home?"

"Yea." He answered as if embarrassed.

"Nice." The kitchen was the size of our kitchen and living room combined.

"Thanks." He flashed me a smile and then grabbed a bottle of *Evian* water from the fridge and we walked upstairs onto the ground floor, past double doors that opened onto other rooms, up another flight of stairs towards the front of the house where his bedroom was. I didn't know what to expect when he opened the door but given the house, his bedroom was so down to earth. He had a bigger bed than mine, and bigger windows that faced onto the street. On the floor near the bed, were several piles of books. On the far side of the room was a desk with a typewriter and loose papers next to it. The walls had black and white posters of people I didn't recognise, and there was a cork board near his closet door that had pink triangle buttons and other political looking stuff. The room was inviting and a reflection of the Si I was getting to know. I stood there not knowing where to move as he went to the windows and closed the thick curtains that looked like they belonged on a stage. He then turned the bedside lamp, adding a glow to the room that made me feel safe. We were alone at last, no world, no friends, just us.

He walked back over to me and ran a finger from my cheek to my chin. I looked up at him, into his eyes before closing them as our lips connected. I wrapped my arms around him tight as our tongues danced. Each motion sent an intense feeling up and down my body. My hands found their way under his shirt and they must have felt cold because he jolted a bit but never stopped kissing. He put his hands up my shirt and the coolness of his touch made me jump in a good way. The shirts soon came off, thrown in opposite directions. Our bare chests were against one another. Si had a cute little patch of hair in the center that I could feel against my smooth chest. He had a tone to his chest and arms that reinforced our age difference. I had never felt my dick so hard and could feel his rubbing against my body. He kissed my ear, letting the feeling linger there as he went lower against my neck, down to my chest, kissing my nipples before coming back up to my lips and meeting my tongue again. I copied what he did to me, not sure how to do anything else but figuring that it was a good start. He took a step back towards the bed and I paced with him till the back of his knees touched the mattress and with a push, he fell backwards, me on top of him. Our hard-ons were pressed against one another and a little sweat developed that felt like it was making our chests stick together, becoming one.

We continued kissing until Si rolled us over. Now he was on top me. He pulled himself up a few inches. His hair was hanging down and there was a sexy look in his eyes before he went back to kissing my neck, working down my chest except this time going further down and kissing my belly button, his tongue continued downward to the waistline. He unbuttoned my shorts, revealing my underwear and rubbing his face against the outline of my dick, making me squirm, and pulling my leg up to get me shorts off easier.

My hematite fell from its pocket; Si picked it up and put it on the night stand. He kissed me on the lips and said, "A gift from James?"

I nodded.

He reached into his shorts and pulled out a near identical one. "James is a sweetheart." He put his next to mine.

He then lowered my underwear, looking up at me as my cock hit his face; he smiled and took me in his mouth. My body jolted with a sensation beyond anything I had ever felt or even imagined when I used to look at those magazines under my mattress. Just when I thought I would come, he pulled away and returned to kissing me. We rolled over and I found myself on top of him, kissing him again, working my way down and wanting to see what I could feel against me. I unbuttoned his shorts, lowered them and his boxers at the same time. I stood up, taking them completely off and looked down at Si who was now naked before me, his uncut cock stood as if at attention and his low hanging balls, laid there just above his crack which had light hairs around it. I went to go down but instead he led me to lay with my head to his crotch and vice versa; so we could both suck at the same time. No amount of imagination on my part could have imagined how good that would feel and I couldn't hold back my excitement which took Si by surprise. As I came, I tried to suck but could only stroke his cock and not too long after I could feel drops against my skin as he came onto my hand.

I stretched out on my back, breathing hard. I could hear Si doing the same and his hand reached towards mine, he pulled himself up, turned around and laid with his head on my chest. I kissed his sweat drenched head, he looked up at me and kissed me; I could taste the salt on his lips. We laid like that for a few minutes before getting under the covers. He put his arms around me like we were spoons and said "that was hot." I agreed with a moan and he kissed me on the neck which made me hard again. I sank into his arms, never wanting to be outside of them.

SUNDAY, JUNE 6, 1993

When I woke up, Si wasn't in bed. I put my shorts on
and heard noise coming from downstairs so I went
down and found him in the kitchen. He was putting
two cups of coffee and some chocolate donuts on a
tray.

He turned around and smiled. His hair was
dishevelled and he was only in his boxers; looking even
cuter than he did the night before. "I was gonna
surprise you." He said.

I caught a glimpse of the time on the microwave
and it felt like the room got darker, as if the storm
clouds had set in. "Fuck, is that the time?"

No matter how many times I looked away and
looked back, it still said, "12.30."

"Your mom's gonna be pissed, huh?"

108

"You may never see me again." I was convinced it would be my last day on Earth.

He walked over and put his arms around me. "I'll wait." He then kissed me on the lips, providing a brief light in the darkness. "Sit."

I took a seat on one of the stools and he stood on the other side of the counter. He passed me a donut and a cup of coffee. We ate breakfast together, postponing the inevitable separation ahead of us, but for that moment none of it mattered. This space was safe and together it seemed like anything was possible.

The air was cooler than it had been the last few days as we walked towards the *Natural History Museum*, to 81st Street subway station entrance. Si gave me a big hug and made me promise to call him to let him know I got home or he would call me. What could have been a threat sounded more like a promise out of concern and there was a nice feeling that rose within me as I took in his words. Each step down the stairs felt like a march towards a death sentence. I looked up from the bottom and he was still there. He pushed his hair back with his hands and blew me a kiss. I sent one back and he waved before heading off.

I pulled my walkman out of my bag and pressed play as I waited for the train to take me uptown, back home to whatever fate laid before me. Bryan Adams' "Summer of 69" started playing and it made me think of the night before even though it was 1993. If today was the last day of my life, yesterday had been the best.

When I got home, there she was sitting in the kitchen. A fire burning in her dark eyes. Without even a blink she asked, "*¿Que hora* you call this?" There was no trace of maternal softness in her voice, just anger, an anger I had never seen. My body shivered at the sound of her words. The freedom of the last twenty four hours was a distant dream. I was home and the gritty surroundings did not lie.

"Um 2'o clock?" I knew that was not the correct response but I couldn't help it. The words had left my mouth before I had had time to think about them.

"*YO SE LA HORA*...don't you get smart with me....Where were you?"

Fear gripped me and I couldn't move my legs. I longed to be back out there with Si, with people who actually got me, who were like me. Anywhere but here.

"Um, um."

She got up from the chair and came right up to my face. "*Mijo*, tell me where you were?" She scanned my face as if she were collecting information from the lines and pores."Are you on drugs?"

My body was shaking now and tears started rolling down my cheeks, "NO" I shouted. I knew that was a lie but honestly, any drugs I had in my system had been replaced with fear.

"Then what? ¡¡¡*Digame*!!!"

My head was spinning. I didn't want to say it. I couldn't say it. I didn't have a grandmother like James. Where would I go? She reached down to take off her *chancleta* with "Puerto Rico" embossed on the leather

111

strap. That slipper instilled fear into me as it did generations of Puerto Rican children. Truth was never far from its sight.

She held it in her hand, ready to extract the truth with one thwack. "*Te pregunto una vez mas*...Where...were...you?"

Through tear stained eyes, the words came out as if they were being spoken by someone else. "Ma, I'm gay!"

Thwack!

"Ow, Ma!!!"

"*¡Eso no es una razon para no llarmame!*"

"What?"

"You heard me! That is no reason not to call. Do you know what I went through last night??? DO YOU???"

"I'm sorry, what was I supposed to say?"

"¡*La verdad!* The way you were raised." She went to walk away, then stopped and turned around. She looked at me with a face of hurt and confusion. "Mi *hermano,* your uncle was gay. Did I ever turn my back on him?"

In that one moment, the look in her eyes made me feel ashamed and selfish. I was luckier than I had ever thought with her as my mom; and the guilt of what I had put her through last night made me nauseous.

"No. But I thought because..."

"Because you are my son, it would be different?"

I nodded, unable to speak the word yes.

"You're right, it is. All I want is for you to be happy, whatever you choose."

"Ma, it's not a choice!"

"Ay yes, I know. Jose used to correct me all the time...*oigame no me importas que eres gay, solamente que sea feliz.* That you're happy!"

She walked towards me again and put her arms around me, holding me tight as if she was trying to cradle the child inside of me; her little boy. She then pulled away, looked at me, wiped the tears from my eyes with her fingers and said, "*Bueno*, tell me about your night?" Her eyes made me think she hadn't been ready to ask that question but then I don't think either of us thought that my coming out was a conversation we were going to have that weekend.

She made us both *cafe con leche* and I told her about meeting Si, the group, meeting Cuchi and James, what happened with Anthony and Melanie and going to the club. I left out the pot smoking and sex because I wasn't stupid.

She listened, nodded in places and I could see was trying to understand while remaining calm that her son had ditched school and gone downtown. There was tenderness in her smile though that told me she was happy for me, that there were no secrets between us. I broke down about the bullying. Why I hated school. Each secret released my body from the chains it had become used to. I could see there was a sadness that her little boy was growing up but she tried her best to not show it.

The phone rang and she got up to answer it. "Hello...Lu? *¿Que?* Ah yes, Luis is here. Who is this?" She looked at me with a mischievous smile and the tone in her voice became playful. "Ah Simon, yes, Lu has told me all about you." Her amusement of my nickname was patronizing.

The color of my cheeks must have been bright red because my face felt like it was on fire as she continued to speak. "No, no it's okay, well it's not but its fine. Are you free next Friday? *Bueno*...good...you come to ours for dinner...no is not an option." Her Latin persistence would always win. "Okay, I will let Lu tell you the time." She smiled as she handed me the phone. My face was filled with teenage horror as she left the kitchen satisfied; giving me some privacy.

"I am so embarrassed, so sorry."

"That was surreal." He responded. The sound of his voice made everything okay.

"So I was gonna see what you were up too next week but I guess we already have plans."

"Looks that way." We both giggled as there was no other response to my mother's invitation.

"I had the best time Lu, best night of my life. Can I see you before Friday?" He asked the question as if he was unsure about the response but hopeful that it would be yes.

I sighed because I knew that no matter how well things were going with mom, I was still in trouble. "I'd love too but I have to ask my mom first." The response was even lamer in words than it was in my thoughts.

"Of course, yes, sure, just let me know." He paused and there was softness in his voice that made me feel like the luckiest person in the world when he said "Can't wait to see you again, Lu."

"Me too...bye Si."

I put the phone down and was smiling from the inside out. Nothing could take away the feeling he gave me. When I looked up, my mother was there. I don't know how long she had been standing there or what she heard but before I could utter a word, she said, "Gay or not, you broke the rules! You're grounded for the week!"

My heart sank. I knew the next week would feel like an eternity. I felt the freedom rings under my shirt and smiled knowing that at least Si would be at the end of this rainbow.

FRIDAY, JUNE 10, 1993

My mother hadn't been completely unreasonable during the week I was grounded. I may not have been able to go downtown or get home later than 4pm but she did let me speak to Cuchi, James and Si every day. It wasn't enough though to hear his voice. I wanted to hold him, kiss him and feel his body again. Each day felt like I was counting down a prison sentence but without the abuse I had had before. Anthony and Melanie *fucking* Sputano stayed away from me although I could see in Anthony's eyes that it was a struggle not to say something. I hadn't felt that powerful before and it was all down to Cuchi.

I looked at my watch after combing my hair in the mirror. Though we hadn't seen each other in nearly a week, what if he didn't like the way I looked anymore?

I decided to mess it up with my hands after combing it. *Such a dork*, I thought to myself. *Ugh.*

I put on my 80's mix tape. "Take On Me" played and that started to calm my nerves. I changed out of the black jeans I had on and opted or blue jeans. I changed the red shirt I had on for a dark blue one which gave me the illusion of a chest. I ruffled my hair once more with my hands and looked in the mirror again. *Yes!*

My mother walked in as I was moving my hips to A-Ha.

"*Mijo.* You going to comb your hair?"

Are you? I wanted to say but first it made no sense because her hair was done to perfection, not to high, the length sitting just below the shoulder and sencond, I didn't think my mother would respond well to shade. *Was that shade?*

I sort of half smiled at her. "It is combed Ma."

"Okay." She said. "You better go and meet him."

I had agreed with her that I could meet Si a few minutes before to say hello. She would follow. I turned off my stereo and headed out the door.

There was a weird feeling as I walked out of the building. Two worlds were about to meet. Two of my worlds and I wasn't sure if either of them would be the same again. I turned the corner of the building and headed up to the Grand Concourse. Rather than cross it, I used the subway station to avoid the traffic. A train had just pulled in because the station was full of people exiting from the platforms. I saw Si headed towards the exit I was walking to. I called out to him which made every one look at me. He turned around and he had a smile from ear to ear. He lifted his bangs with his right hand and then waved at me. He looked out of place and yet he was right where he needed to be. I got closer and noticed he was wearing khakis, his *Converse*, a green t-shirt and a blue blazer. It was the kind of outfit that would look out of place on me but on him, it looked like the most natural choice. He was holding a large gift bag and I saw some red roses sticking out of them.

"Hey." He said and walked towards me. He put one arm around me to hug me and although I should have jumped because of where we were. I hugged him back. I looked around but no one had noticed us hug.

"Those for me?" I asked.

He blushed. "Yes and a bottle of wine for your mom."

"Seriously, they're for me?" I said. "I was only teasing."

"Of course they are. It'd be a bit weird giving your mom red roses."

I had never received flowers. Could men give each other flowers? "Yea, I guess."

He giggled and we headed towards the exit that would take us to *El Chino*.

"You look cute." He said and bumped into me.

"So do you." I responded and bumped him back.

The doubts I had earlier disappeared and the long week without seeing him had come to an end. There was no distance between us.

My mother was at the top of the stairs waiting for us. She was looking around unsure and had a nervous expression. I hadn't thought how strange it would be for her. I called out to her from halfway up the stairs and she smiled at me. She then looked at Si and back at me. I couldn't tell what that meant.

When we got to the top of the stairs, I introduced them. Si handed the bag to my mother. She looked at it then back at him.

"Umm, Mrs. Morales, I brought you a bottle of wine and the flowers are for Lu. I hope that's okay."

She looked in the bag and then patted me on the arm. "*Ay Luis, tienes un caballero aqui, no?*"

"*Claro.*" I looked at him. "Let's talk in English though Ma."

"*Ay* yes." She said. "Thank you very much Simon."

"You're welcome."

She grabbed him by the arm. "I speak the first word that comes to mind, sometimes English, sometimes Spanish. Sometimes both."

"It's okay." He said and looked at me then at her. "My mother and I do that with French."

"*Bueno*. Good."

I held the door to *El Chino* open for them. It was a sight to see, Si and my mother. My two worlds together.

Hector Chan greeted us inside and my mother gave him a big hug. I saw her whisper something to him. He looked at me then her and then Si. He extended his hand to Si and then came up to me and gave me a very strong hug.

"I told you you reminded me of your Uncle." He said which made me turn red. "*No te preocupes*, that's not a bad thing."

He then grabbed both Si and I by the arms. "Everyone is welcome here." He looked at my mother. *"Mi familia."*

Hector showed us to our usual table and told us the first round of drinks were on the house. My mother had a Piña Colada, both Si and I had iced tea. Si looked at the menu and we pretended to look at it. My mother gave me her secret joke smile which made me laugh and Si look up.

"Everything okay?" He asked.

"Yea." I said. "We always order the same thing so there's no point in us looking at the menu but we always do. Just a stupid joke."

He put his menu down and looked at us relieved. "Me too. Hot & sour soup, egg roll, pork fried rice and sweet & sour pork."

My mother laughed and I could see Si relax. I had only ever seen him in his environment where he was confident and cool. Seeing him nervous made me feel less like a dork for being nervous around him or anywhere.

My mother reached over and patted his hand. "Relax *mijo*. This is supposed to be a fun night to get to know you."

He looked at me and I nodded my head to say *it's all cool.*

Hector returned with our drinks and my mother proposed a toast.

"To new friends."

We clinked our glasses and Hector took our orders.

My mother folded her hands in front of her and leaned in towards Si like she was interviewing him for a job.

"So Simon, Luis says you study French at NYU. What do you want to do when you graduate?"

"Um." Si looked at me and then my mother. "I don't know yet. Maybe teach or something."

"How old are you?"

"Turned 19 this past May."

"Ma." I said.

"*Mijo.* I just want to make sure the age is not too big. Okay?"

"It's okay." Si said. "She's right to ask."

My mother looked pleased with his response. He seemed to know the right thing to say.

"Do your parents know you are." She hesitated. "Gay?"

"They do Mrs. Morales and they are totally cool with it."

She put her arm around me. "Good. *Bueno.* I don't want my son to be a secret. He deserves to have someone proud to be with him.

I put my head on her shoulder. "Thanks, Ma."

Si's eyes met mine and I could see his hand move like he wanted to reach out towards me. He stopped and looked at my mother.

"Mrs. Morales. I would be proud and happy if Lu wanted to be with me."

"I do." I said.

"*Mijo calmate*. Let's not rush into marriage just yet ok."

Si laughed and I felt embarrassed but it broke the interview tension of the conversation just in time for our appetizers.

"I mean I would, I want."

"Okay Okay." My mother said. "*Aprovechen*. Eat."

By the time the main meals came, there was no tension or weirdness at the table. I could tell my mother liked Si and I was happy that my worlds were becoming one instead of clashing. He told her about

127

Paris and London which I could see in her face excited her in the same way it excited me. A whole other world that existed on TV or in books for us. He spoke of his parents who were away most weekends but they had complete trust in him.

I got a little sad when our plates had been cleared because I knew that meant that our night was coming to an end and I didn't want Si to go. I wanted to find a way to hold him or kiss him.

My mother looked at me. "*Ay mijo*. Why so serious?"

I shook my head.

She looked at me and then at Si who didn't know where to look.

I decided to take a chance. "Can I stay at Si's tomorrow night?"

She took a deep breath. "I don't know. Simon, can Luis stay at yours tomorrow?"

Si's face lit up. "Only if it is okay with you Mrs. Morales."

"He's not grounded tomorrow so yes that is fine *pero* Sunday, I want you home in time to do your homework. Okay?"

"Thank you Ma." I kissed her on the cheek.

"Tonight. Simon can sleep on the sofa."

I looked at both of them. *Was she serious?*

"Oh no, its okay Mrs Morales. I can take the subway home."

My mother put her hand up. "At this *hora*. No, if something happened to you. *No.* I couldn't forgive myself."

Si looked at me. "Oh okay. *Gracias.*"

"*De nada.*"

Hector Chan gave us all big hugs when we left and the three of us headed back to the apartment. When we got in, I got some spare sheets, pillow and blanket for Si. My mother gave us a few minutes to say goodnight.

"Thank you for coming."

He held my hand. "Your mom is cool."

I looked up.

"Yea, I guess she is."

We looked into each other's eyes. I couldn't not kiss him goodnight. What was supposed to be a quick kiss turned into a full on tongue session till my mother yelled from the other room.

"That's enough."

Si and I laughed and I kissed his hand before heading to my bedroom. I couldn't wait till the morning and for whatever the rest of the weekend had in store for us.

MONDAY JUNE 28, 1993

I didn't want to get out of bed. I didn't want the weekend to end. I was still feeling the energy of marching down Fifth Avenue in my first ever Pride parade. It was like nothing I could ever imagine. Si and holding hands down the middle of Fifth Avenue as we were cheered on by people on both sides of the street. Okay, they may have been cheering Cuchi on more as she was dressed in a full length rainbow gown that had a train that was held up by some wire so it looked like she was gliding down the road.

I lost count the amount of pictures we posed for and after it was done we hung out on the piers to the early morning. My mother had given me special permission to stay with Si on a Sunday night since the last day of school was just a formality and the teachers would let us out early.

Si had set his alarm for me but I had snoozed it a few times. There was a sliver of sunlight coming through his bedroom curtains and it was just on his back. He was laid on his front with one arm around me. There were remnants of glitter in his hair and on his shoulders.

The alarm went off again and he tapped me on the chest.

"Alright Lu, c'mon." He said. "You don't want to start the summer grounded."

That was true. As cool as my mom had been, I was still afraid of rocking the boat too much.

"Okay." I said. "5 more minutes."

Five minutes turned into ten and then I jumped into the shower and afterwards got dressed.

"You sure you want to wear that shirt?" Si asked. "Especially where you are going."

I had been thinking about the last day of school
since I came out. With Anthony and Melanie no longer
harassing me, most people just left me alone. They
weren't friendly but they weren't mean either. Each
day I was out, I was becoming more proud and I hated
hiding it. As much as I wanted to wear my *I'm not gay
but my boyfriend is* t-shirt from *Don't Panic,* I settled on
the 2QT2BSTR8 t-shirt instead. I figured it was funny
but most of all, the kids at school wouldn't get it any
way. It would require them to acknowledge me in
order to read it. I put on a flannel shirt over it to make
Si comfortable but left it unbuttoned.

I looked at him and smiled. "Yea. It's time."

He walked me to the subway station and made a
comment about the buttons on my school bag. I had a
pink triangle, a rainbow flag pin and two male symbols
interlinked. I could tell in his voice, he was worried.

"It's cool, I know what I am doing." I said. I didn't
but whatever was about to happen, I wanted to face it.

He hugged me tight at the station and kissed me on the neck. The thrill of seeing that many gay people on the streets of New York made me feel safe as we said goodbye, even though Monday was just another day in the city.

I listened to a Pride mix tape that Si had made for me a week before the parade. It had the classics like *It's Raining Men, I Am What I Am, I Will Survive and I'm Coming out.* Each song made me feel happier and happier as I headed to school for the final day of the year.

When I got to Westchester Square, I started to feel a little panic as I felt people were looking at my school bag but when I turned to see, no one was paying attention to me. I continued up the hill towards the school with my headphones on. "A Deeper Love" was playing on my Walkman. I stopped in front of the building. I could tell the second bell had already rung because the terrace was empty apart from a few late comers like me.

I put my headphones back on and walked up the stairs and headed to the entrance. I continued to look ahead without meeting anyone's eyes. I was the last one to arrive in home room and since my seat was in the middle of the room, I had to walk past most of the class. I kept my headphones on and my bag with the buttons was visible to the room. When I sat down, I turned my Walkman off and let my headphones rest around my neck. I looked ahead of the room still afraid to look at anyone. I wondered to myself what the fuck had I just done. I looked around the room and most of the class had not even paid attention to me. They were in their little groups as usual unaware of my presence.

Mrs. Napolitano told us that the school was gonna let us out half day. The teachers were eager to start their summer vacation as much as the students. She looked at my bag and smiled at me before dismissing us.

When I got up, one of the girls in my class wished me a happy summer. We had been in the same classes all year long and she had said nothing to me. After that a few other of my classmates did the same. I took my flannel shirt off and put it in my school bag.

The rest of the morning, I got a few looks but no one said anything. I saw Melanie *fucking* Sputano pull Anthony to one side when I walked past him. I thought I heard him say *he's fucking rubbing it in my face now* but I could have imagined it. The anxiety I had when I got off the subway that morning had faded and I don't know if it was because it was the last day of school and no one cared or if they really didn't care but no one said anything bad to me. In fact, people took notice.

I didn't want to push my luck so I walked out of the school before last period of the morning. I didn't feel my education would suffer from having missed gym class. The terrace was busy as it seemed others had the same idea as me. I looked around and half waved and smiled at students, some did the same back. It felt like I was the ghost that people started to see.

When I got to the stairs of the main entrance, I saw him standing across the street by the bus stop.

I ran across the street.

"What are you doing here?"

"I just wanted to make sure you were okay." Si said. He had his hands in his shorts pockets. There was still a sparkle to his hair from the glitter but it just added to his magic.

"I am now."

I put my arms around him and hugged him.

"What do you want to do now?" He asked.

I looked at him and then the subway.

"Let's go home." I said. "Downtown."

"I thought you might say that." He responded. "I told Cuchi and James to meet us on the pier."

I smiled and we headed towards the subway station. I didn't look back at the school, I just kept looking forward. I could only see good things ahead.

ABOUT THE AUTHOR

John Lugo-Trebble was born and raised in The Bronx. He
He now lives in Cornwall with his husband David and their
three cats; a long way from Christopher Street.

His work has appeared in *Jonathan: A Queer Fiction Journal*,
Litro Magazine and others.

You can find out more about him and his work at
www.johnlugotrebble.com

Printed in Poland
by Amazon Fulfillment
Poland Sp. z o.o., Wrocław

54846944R00089